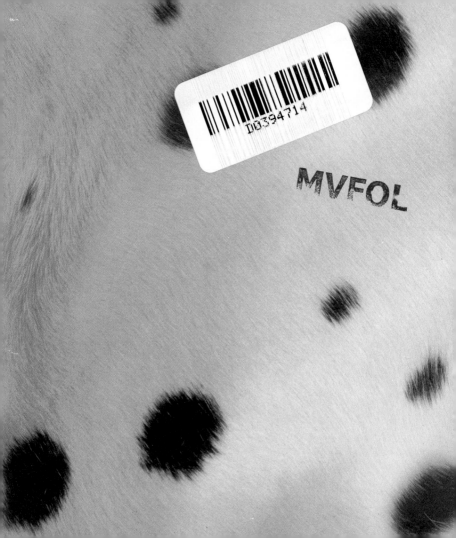

Goldilocks &
The Three Bears

Adapted by Bill Shockey
Illustrated by James Finch

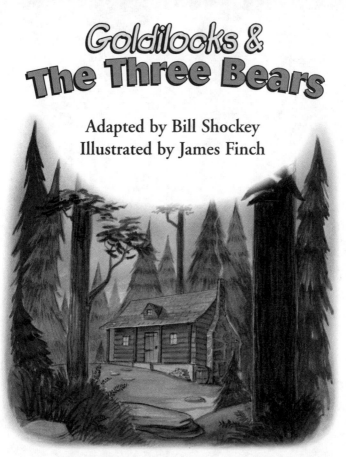

Art Directed by Shannon Osborne Thompson and Lanaye Melton
Edited by Jan Keeling

Once upon a time there were three bears: a great big Papa Bear, a middle-sized Mama Bear, and a little Baby Bear.

One morning Mama Bear made some porridge for breakfast, but it was much too hot to eat. The three bears decided to go for a walk while their porridge cooled on the table.

Nearby in the forest, a young girl named Goldilocks became lost while she was picking flowers. As she wandered about, she saw the cozy little cottage that was the home of the three bears. She tried the front door and found that it was not locked.

Goldilocks entered the door and saw the three bowls of porridge on the table. "Oh, I am very hungry, and it smells so good," the little girl said out loud.

She tasted a spoonful of porridge from the big bowl and said, "This is much too hot!"

Then she took a bite from the middle bowl of porridge and said, "This is much too cold!"

Then she took a spoonful out of the smallest bowl. "Mmm," she said, "this one is just right," and she ate up all the porridge.

Goldilocks saw
three chairs by
the fireplace.
She thought,
"I am very tired and
would like to rest by
the warm fire."

First she sat in Papa Bear's chair. "This chair is much too big for me!" she cried. She next sat in Mama Bear's chair and said, "This chair is much too wide for me!"

Then she sat in the smallest chair that belonged to Baby Bear and said, "Oh, this chair is just right." But all of a sudden the chair broke, and she fell to the floor with a bang!

Then Goldilocks thought, "I am very sleepy and would like to take a nap." She climbed the stairs to find a place to rest and found three beds.

She first tried Papa Bear's bed. "This bed is much too hard for me!" she said.

Then she tried Mama Bear's bed and said, "This bed is much too soft for me!"

Next, Goldilocks lay down on Baby Bear's bed. "Ah, this bed is just right," she said, and she fell fast asleep.

Just about this time the three bears came home from their walk.
They knew right away that someone had been in their cottage.

"Someone has been eating my porridge," said Papa Bear. "Someone has been eating my porridge," said Mama Bear.

Baby Bear said, "Someone has been eating my porridge, and LOOK, now it is all gone!"

The three bears walked over to the fireplace. "Someone has been sitting in my chair," said Papa Bear. "Someone has been sitting in my chair," said Mama Bear.

Baby Bear said, "Someone has been sitting in my chair, and LOOK, now it is all broken!"

The three bears quietly went up the stairs. Papa Bear took one look at his bed and said, "Someone has been sleeping in my bed." Mama Bear said, "Someone has been sleeping in my bed." Baby Bear said, "Someone has been sleeping in my bed, and LOOK, there she is!"

Suddenly Goldilocks woke up from her nap and saw the three bears. She jumped out of the bed, went down the stairs as fast as she could, and ran right out the door. And the three bears NEVER saw Goldilocks again.

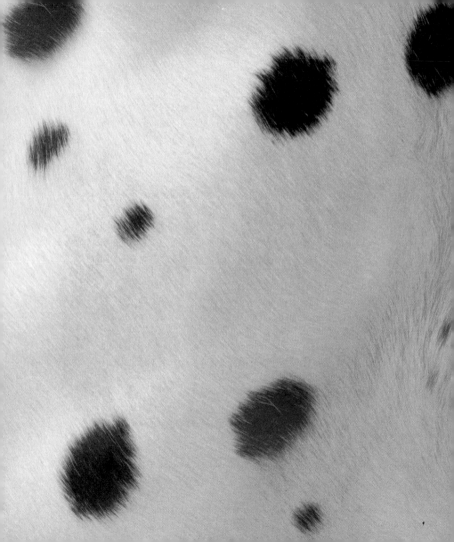